INTROVERT THE STORYTELLER

MANVI

Made with ♥ on the Notion Press Platform
www.notionpress.com

Contents

Preface

This book contain a number of anecdotes based on life experience of an introvert who loves to change herself in a right way. Who don't want to suffer with her silly overthinking and flaws.

This Introvert promise you readers to give more short stories , anecdotes, poems and Novella .you just have to read and enjoy the series '*Introvert – The Storyteller*'

If you find any fault in my writing; still got the meaning of it...

This book contain a number of anecdotes based on life experience of an introvert who loves to change herself in a right way. Who don't want to suffer with her silly overthinking and flaws.

This Introvert promise you readers to give more short stories , anecdotes, poems and Novella .you just have to read and enjoy the series '*Introvert – The Storyteller*'

If you find any fault in my writing; still got the meaning of it...

You are genius and dedicated readers..

After knowing the fact that I made mistakes I had still wrote these stuff..

Just because I love writting

-your. Bohemian.....

Acknowledgements

Want to thanks everyone who for their existing in my movie like life

thanks .

CHAPTER ONE

Birthday gift

This story is from my sweetest and mischievous childhood. When I was of eight and my brother was one year younger than me . We lived in Gwalior with our parents, in a rented room a small kitchen was also attached to it .

One morning , a lady came to our room who was our neighbor and my mom's friend. Me and my brother were playing we just greeted her and restart playing . We didn't give her any attention but when she ate our favorite biscuits my all attention was shifted from game to her .After drinking a cup of tea and a plateful biscuits she gave us invitation of her daughter's birthday party on same evening.

When she want back we ask mom several times what she said . But mom didn't tell us anything about evening party .

It was around eleven in morning ,she went to a gift shop and brought a pair of dolls as a birthday present for that birthday girl. And strictly warned us not to touch the dolls but again she didn't mention any reason why not to touch them .

We were we ,while mom was taking afternoon nap .we took pair of dolls from cupboard . I along with my trouble creating partner (My brother) enter in our kitchen from there we took a mugful water and Dish wash, we bring it to bedroom and sit there near door. Finally we unwrapped doll and rub soap to its face ,body then my brother gave water and I squeeze beautiful brown hair of doll .

Listening to our Whispers mom suddenly waked up and saw the soap water going out through space under door. She searched us on both side of her as we were not in bed she sat immediately on bed and notice that we were putting pins on doll's body in order to stick clothes .

The moment when we realized that she was staring us ,we got startled and packed doll as quickly as possible for us.

In evening mom give me envelope of money to give birthday girl. When I asked her- "why not dolls ?"

She gave horrific look to me by increasing her eye ball size .

My brother was intelligent enough to understand the delicateness of moment so he went out quietly.

But I was noob ,and asked her again "why this why not dolls after all we made them clean and ready to attend party".

My mom shout_- "because it wasn't a **birthday gift** anymore".

CHAPTER TWO

Learning piano

This is a part of my Introvert teenage when I study in eighth, speaking with people around me was challenging task for me especially with teachers ,boys, strangers, whenever there is any case in which I have to face them I used to behave like it is a great mission and I am confronting terrorist .

There was a time when I want to say my music teacher that I am interested in learning piano. But I don't have gut to speak in front of whole class . So I started searching chance to speak her about my strong desire to learn piano. Before and after assembly ,during recess, in free period or after school over I often search chance but I failed several times.

One day after school over I courageously told my music teacher about my deep heated wish . She politely suggested me to join class next day or in any free period of mine .It wasn't as difficult as I made it by overthinking .

Well. On next day I reached there . I entered and talked to her a bit more than before she instructed me in nice way slightly my confidence boost. And I started pressing keys as per her orders.

I was playing well enough suddenly my dance teacher and music teacher notice me and I became conscious and nervous and stopped pressing keys. Looking this my music teacher scold me a bit .

Then what ! I never went their again I pretend again and again that she is bad ,rude , arrogant and what not . It was all my stupid ego which made me get apart from piano.

It was that day when I left opportunity to learn and it's today when I am dying to touch piano keys ,guitar and other instruments.

"So never be so stupidly egoistic that your negative ego took the moment when you're leaving for your dreams".

CHAPTER THREE

My Cute Porrifera

My all maths teacher were dangerous and hypercritic .I still remember how they slap me and pull my cheeks so tightly until it became red and when she realise it seems she didn't stop pulling.

I had many mathematics teacher from juniors to inter (12th) But one teacher who is very close to my heart is my cute Porrifera....

She was my class teacher in ninth standard and taught mathematics .her name was...one second why should I give free publicity to her ...kidding. When I was in junior class I like her confidence, way of taking and dressing sense . When ever I saw her in morning my day goes well ,but when she became our class teacher .All the favor which I had for her turned into negative .

Truly, I am accepting that I am poor in mathematics. My performance wasn't good enough and this was the plus point for her to give taunt and insult me. she never miss any chance. Whenever She started checking our notebook I got horrified ,while checking she used to call my name and mark small and big circles in my notebook with red pen there was a time when my notebook contain more mistakes than questions and solution .Finding fault in notebook was okay for me I was ready to accept that notebook but it was hard for her to digest with out taunting me .

Let me share a incident it was notebook checking day and she was going to ask formulas in first period I was terrified by this and started crying in assembly. My English teacher saw me weeping and ask me reason I didn't tell her.

I started disliking her and gave her name rigid, 'Porrifera' (porrifera is term in biology it was hard to understand and remember she was too captious so I named her). Me with my friend criticize her .

Somehow the year passed, I get rid of her . The Euphoria of being free from that teacher was indescribable .

One day ,when I was in 11th standard I was going to school in midway she stopped her scotty and said me to sit behind her . I was emotional less there were many questions rolling my head just me ..why just me??there were other children too. In school when she stopped her vehicle I too get off . She smiled and moved. That day I decided to forgive her bad behavior in past with me .

Again I started liking her confidence, dressing sense and smile .But this time I humbly request god not to resend her back in my life. I think '**My cute Porrifera'** is still creating mess in life of '**my juniors'.**

CHAPTER FOUR

London Street of my dream

I several times travelled through narrow streets, both side sides of street there was maple trees the narrow path was filled with dry maple leaves and red flowers .I was alone in street walking and humming my favorite song . Well this happens every time I my fantasy world. Reality is just opposite of my all imaginations. But there was a narrow street near my home it is not so soul soothing .but my imagination is enough to make it beautiful route for me.

When I was in tenth I used to travel through that street it became memorable street for me there is a story behind it .

I went for science and maths tuition from there . I am sure you started yawning while reading science and maths in mid of such story well same here !

I like such type of street I have a dream to visit London's narrow streets and arcade.

Although it was filled with swamps during rainy season.some time excreta of cattles and dirty water over flowed from canals . But my imagination can turn such shabby place into captivating one. I used to play live Subway surfer by hopping and stepping on stones still it was my favorite way .

One day while coming back to home there was a man standing with his bike .he had horizontally parked his bike and continuously staring me . Street was narrow and I was very close to him when I came across my heart was pounding.Infact in night I was thinking about it . These things repeated daily. Whenever I cross through road I found him there .

One day I told it to mom she send my brother with me . Bu there was no one on that day .Next day when I was alone I saw him again.

This time mom advised me to come through another route which was long but according to her it was safe . But it took fifteen minutes extra and by London Street I reached within five minutes.

So I decided to came through same street but this time I carry stone and unemployed brother of compass(divider) with me . I started watching self defence video but never get any thing from them. And a another video in which a lawyer was advising girls that you can hit someone if you feel he can harm you . But you don't have to kill him .

Well after sometime everything became normal neither I change my route nor he make me horrified anymore.

That street taught me by changing route I can't eliminate such people.

If you think you can change your way to avoid them than listen they too can chance there way just to make you fright from them.

At last I want to thank unemployed brother of compass for empowering me . Now you tell me who was that?

CHAPTER FIVE

Insecurities....

Introvertness and insecurities were two best friends who used to live in my traits. Me as a introvert was very conscious about my hair's, my skin, my nails, my clothes and what not.

Here I am sharing some of stories related to all these insecurities which I experienced in my past. Now I am a Philomath but there was a time, when I small And senseless things made me cry bitterly.

There is a story related to my finger and nails when I was in 8th standard I used to go to school by school bus. There was a girl who was elder from me I used to call her sister inverted commas she had beautiful fingers and long nails which seem attractive to me I wish to have seen but my fingers were not so thin and I have a small nails so I decided you cut my nails for one or two months. And one more thing was that I decided to add 2 chapattis instead of three and I decided to cut my meal so that I could make my fingers and body slim and thin. You'll consider it a stupid idea I also agree now but that time I call it a good idea and follow it up to one week.

Days passed and I feel uncomfortable by my increased nails because of dirt and grease which again and again made them look untidy and make me feel irritated. At last I cut all my nails and from that day I hate long nails it's so creepy to maintain them and again and again I started eating 3 chapatis again but that's not a happy ending. There were many incidents with me which make me insecure about my looks and stuff.

Like my hairs, that special kind of hers which God gift me as a gift are so extraordinary that I have no words to describe them I used to thought that whenever I will meet any girl who have same hairs like mine I'm going to ask her about her hair care routine. My hair are rough in fact they are very rough if you saw me without combing my hair you got scared of me. My mom always liked to compare me with other girls she always turns me that other girls of my age and or younger than me know how to style their hairs how to make different kind of hairstyles and I don't know anything. This is now not a new thing to me. It happens with me from very young age. And I think mostly of you had suffered this too.So one day I decided to make a hairstyle of my rough hairs I open a video on Internet and learn to make side braids then I paused video and start making my bread but you can't imagine how badly my hair Tangled firstly I tried to separate them gently but they didn't. I was tried after some time the untangled here make me angry and break my patience and I comb them harshly as a result a lot of hair broke down and I cry for half an hour by tapping my feet on the floor As forcefully as I can. Now if anybody asks me what I gain by doing that so I will answer nothing. My stupidity was next level which every time embraced me. And the level of anger always harm me there was a lot of thing which I lose just because of my anger.

Another thing which make me feel insecure was comments of cute people around me. I'm writing them cute because I can't call them dogs and cats. because I respect my elders. But they always say me dear take a strong rod. Embedded it into walls near the door. Hang on it with empty stomach in morning it will increase your height.

They advise me to drink complain till now seriously without knowing how healthy it is! That time I got hurted by their comments on me but now I take it easy. My height is short so the clothes which I wear hang on me. They are loose and my father used to buy large size clothes for me as he thought I'm going to grow but his genuine thinking make me uncomfortable every time.

When I was in 9th standard. We have to wear track suits in our school as we had become seniors white pants for Wednesday and Saturday wasn't allowed anymore

As usual my father bought a size bigger than my actual size and height. I was very glad that I have to wear tracksuit now. But now when I wore it. It make me feel uncomfortable and insecure I I did triple fold of my lower from upside and double fold of my track. Perhaps teacher commented me that I brought over size in front of whole class. How embarrassing it was! In front of whole Class A introvert receives such comment which made her insecure as much as nobody can feel. My younger brother is taller than me and that tracksuit didn't fit him. Now you can imagine what I had worked that day and how it was looking on me.

Even today if I try my old clothes they are not fit still. And according to my father's calculation about my height and my clothes selection Reality is contrasting.

So now I left to imagine myself in a good costume. I have gained confidence like celebrities and models who always wear anything which seems weird to us but they put confidently on them and walk like a person this who didn't care about the captious people around them.

CHAPTER SIX

Backbencher

IWas a backbencher. I'm still a backbencher and I love to sit there on the last seat. when all best friends are present and maths teacher is absent then it became my day. A backbencher like me should have qualities like not doing shit works which don't have head and foot, backbencher is one who never ever take any stress related to studies but it doesn't mean that backbencher is irresponsible, no it's wrong assumption of your they also cares. They put their effort in their passion. Sometime Backbenchers are talented but teacher never give any attention to them because they don't belong to a there category or you can say they didn't belong to sin Cos Theta family .

But these are qualities of good backbenchers in my past I was a bad backbencher. Bad in terms that are used to criticize Topper cause they are good in maths and science. Although I was also a little bit good but I knew that I don't like to be good in these subjects because for being good I always did rote learning for those things whose meaning or explanation wasn't given by my teachers or you can say I never do good to ask teacher.

But now I didn't criticize stoppers they are already under pressure and I don't want that they do suicide just because of me.

There was a girl whose name was Anushika . she was Topper of my class. My maths teacher appreciate her all the time she had made a timetable and fit it in her watch. Our teacher compared us with her we got irritated by that. Once me and my friend ask her to give her watch and she denied this hurt our stupid ego and we started criticizing her as much as we can every day every hour every minute. How stupid? That time we didn't think that it's her choice to give us watch or not this was one of the bad habit. Now I feel myself guilty for doing that . May be I turned into ethical backbencher.

You know we often say society is judgmental but somewhere we also become part of this hypercritical society. I am backbenchers just because someone criticized me so how can I criticize others. I wish that my Topper could win the race in which they are running. But I love to live outside from such competition ,in a charming and peace full Weather under sun shines and rain drops.

CHAPTER SEVEN

Capital of India ?

We all are truly introduced with nowadays modern and private schools. Most of us are privileged that we are going to school,to learn new things, to make friends and to do study and fun . good friends, good teacher and good books are truly stress buster for every one who feel stressed and hate their life .

Big schools , qualified teachers and facilities which are more than enough like online studying make students more comfortable than before.

Around three decades earlier,there were no such facilities for students. There were few schools and they were also government schools.

My mom, Always tell us about the kind off school in which she had studied .

They were Seven sisters and two brothers . Not all people were open minded there was very little importance of study especially for girls instead of that they all got chance to read unto primary class .

She along with her young sister went to a village school which was two -three kilometers from there home , carrying bad on on side of shoulders and milk can of one litre on other hand They used to ran as fast as possible .there bags were made up of left pieces, when it was extra after striching there suit-salwar tailor used to stich bag with same fabric.

They sprinted in so that they could reach school on time . firstly they have to delever milk can in one of their teachers house which was in opposite direction from school.

Whenever they reached late in school same teacher give them punishment for late entering .

“Next level hypocrisy”.

There were only few teachers , sometime only one teacher came to teach and he asks simple GK questions like-what s capital of India? Whole class became quite because neither they knew nor teachers taught them .but still strict teacher beat them on hand with stick.

During interval,that only teacher went to near tea shop and talks for hours and hours there .

While students ate lunch,went to wash room, drunk water again went to washroom and again drink water . They use to play for left hours.

When teacher came again he ordered peon to rung bell to over school.

There was a month of July which was very special for students and their family because they’d to sown paddy in field. Labors took money .so girl and boy help families and in order to save money families were always agree to keep them in paddy fields. This all happened while crops were harvested .After finishing all work when they rejoined classes.

Then teacher asked them- **‘capital of India???’**

And punished every one for not answering.

CHAPTER EIGHT

How copy cat i was!

Another story from my 8th class life, I was a serious and studious child. You can imagine a child under pressure of everyone who is sincere not because of desire to be that. Just because teacher will cut marks or scold for not being understanding All of them I was a student who used to make notebooks books online , matlab manual, science lab manual and each project or without head foot activities which were given to us only for bothering us.

One day, teacher came into classroom with the news that exams where about to come she provided us date sheet will stop there were a free. And arrangement teacher was sitting in our class. She ordered us to study any subject. So I started reading Hindi then I saw my bench meets we're banding toward each other in a way like they are discussing something. I thought that they were solving mathematics questions. And I realize, how stupid I am as I was reading easiest subject whereas I was weak in maths. So I draw out my rough notebook and maths notebook and start solving questions after 4-5 questions I had a doubt.

Can you solve this query of mine? I asked from them. They turned my side when I looked toward them I saw they were making henna designs on a piece of paper. Then what I put off my maths book and restart doing myself study of other subjects. How copycat I was! I still think that I am a copycat in some important corner of my life people around me are also copycat like my father. Whenever I'm doing something different or creative and show him he always advice me do your study and gain 70% or above than it don't do this useless thing.My teachers, elders, relative every time suggest same thing to me and if I talk something different then they become sarcastic and don't me do whatever you want, spoil your life or future by your hand. I never understand one thing how can they give me guarantee that I Will Survive well and fine in this suffocated present to make future according damn.

Now who will tell them I am bohemian no not a copycat pressurized fellow any more!

CHAPTER NINE

The only blood stream..

Would you like to listen my mensuration experience in this story I'm going to tell you about the only blood Mensuration. It happens with all females from teen age to 40s fifties in short lifelong God gift. Mostly people feel awkward or shy to speak about this especially females. First time when I listen about mensuration at my early teenage I pray to God that if it will not happens with me then I'll become the luckiest girl but after I grown up and had knowledge about this then I get to know that if it does not happens with me then I will not be the luckiest and happiest. Because for biological functioning menstruation should happen every month to every femaleof the particular age group.

First time when it happened with me I was with my aunt. She didn't give me broad information about it. But yes she give basic instructionlike what to do what to wear, how to sit ,what to eat and etc. But when I asked my mom after homecoming she was shocked that's why I'm asking this to her.

BecauseI was just 13 year old and according to her belief and experience menstruation sounds something bad or something which should not happen too earlier stop I seem I believe then because all females whom I know told me that it's a bad irritating thing and females should keep it all private means if they are feeling bad they does not share it with anyone. They keep this matter private. In fact when we go to channel shop to buy sanitary pad shopkeepers wrapped it with newspaperpaper or put it in a black polythene

Back to the story, so I was unaware about the truth that's why it happened to me in early age invite happened with everybody let's stop in one hand I had intelligent questions while on the other hand I was following some rules and regulation which does not add any sense totally meaningless.

I used to live like a spy during my periods I never talk properly to anyone. Always behave like frustrated Zombie, I maintain a special privacy from my father brother. Especially while drawing sanitary pad from cupboard just showing off I didn't have cupboard only have a small attache suitcase my mother gave me as I make dear God butmessy using a separate bucket and soap, using a separate bed sheet and sitting on the floor and one of my favorite myth not worshipping , my favorite because for me God is everywhere and I can talk to God from anywhere. Not only me, these things are followed by every woman including my mom.

Mostly time I notice that women do not know the reason and they bounded by myth and fake beliefs and norms which were passed forward through generations and generation. According to our story which I heard from females who used to live around me a woman in ancient time did something sinful so God girls all women for that. Another story which I heard is that God had gift mensuration to women to reduce their problem. Now think which one is logical obviously move one of them. God is great not cruel or selfish. This painful mensuration happens for a wonderful reason not for this stupid myths.

There was a incident , once i got stain of blood on my school uniform .Teacher scold me by saying -"how can you be so irresponsible" "what if boys saw this they'll laugh on you". That was a small thing but she made it as big like i was criminal or something like that .

One question in my head why boys laugh on me . on the contrary , truth is differ from her beliefs I heard a boy saying , there is no sense in laughing on such situation ,and if some one is laughing then you should feel greatfull that you had increased their blood by showing your stain.

CHAPTER TEN

My dears...

When I was six year old I went to study in a government school of village there I have many friends but when I went to Gwalior My parents Saint me to English medium school.

I was in first standard when I meet my first 2best friends forever they were muskan and zishan. That time muskan and zishan were in second standard our class set parallel to their class. Once my teacher, said to correct my mistake to muskan as she was senior she did correction in my notebook.

She found me cute because of my small coconut tree like pony and I was attracted to her after listening her name Muskan because it was my name in village school

Next year I jumped second class as I was good enough to cover the course of second class. Muskan and I become classmate still we were not friends .

We became best friends by one incident. Actually there was a girl who always got less marks in every test. One day she acquired good marks and it was my idea to do little fun with her by hiding her test paper. I gave it to scan and she thought it was a waste paper and turned it after that she threw it in dustbin.

As a result, teacher put a tight slap on my face as it was my plan. I cried for long time by putting my face down on the desk.

Usually I used to greet her good morning or give her a smiley look but from that day I did not talk to her.

few days later, she came to me and ask apology for all her mistake end request me to be her friend. She was a good dancer grandma I was a nerd. But I always support her in finishing her math's was weak And for me it was my favorite subject that time Muskan always inspire me to participate in dance and music but that time I was interested in maths only. She was sweetest person I ever meet. Once she came to play holi with me andone day when I went to her home she was riding cycle I sat behind her she show me their fields and village. That was a memorable day I'm not going to forget. I wish I could meet her again. Ne

I met zishan in same class. He was a good singer, shy person ,He never talk to anybody else in whole class I don't know why but he is our good friend all of us came together from the school to home. He was my first friend by whom I get to know about the existence of music. Because it wasn't allowed in my home to play music channel.

His voice was magical whenever he asked my match register to complete his work I requested him to sing song in return of it. In evening he came to play with us .

I miss both of them a lot. They were first friends with whom I feel comfortable to share my happy moments. I know that they live very far from my home but still they are very close to my heart. I'm not going to forget them. In any condition if I will suffered from Alzheimer then also there are some people whom I Will not

forget and they are one of them.

CHAPTER ELEVEN

Gratitude to life

I am a traveler person. I don't like wars, enemies, fighting, killing. What I like is sharing my smile with the people who want to smile. Giving ideas to change situation which is desirable vital. Travelling throughout the world here and there and everywhere is one of my dreams. I like to be optimistic like mountain who stand like a warrior, I like serene water of river which is Cool even in worse situations . I like the air which whenever touch my cheek I feel that all positivity of this universe is with me I like birds singing better than me. I love sun which never do any discrimination with me not only with me but with all of us and all the matter in this whole universe. I like crazy activities of my domestic animals which make me smile every time even I was unhappy. I like my friends who always help me to bring positive changes in my life. You know what I feel about this nature it's quite adorable. I can't let it to distract. I thought and hoped that God will give me this life again. But I know it will not going to happen so living this life incredibly it's the only target I have life is first and last don't waste it in arguing complaining combatting or talking useless stuff. Be happy for your own self it's very important she'll need happiness to live or to share it with others

At last I am going to clear one thing. Whatever I wrote in this book is just my views I am not disregarding any one neither teacher nor maths and science.I know teacher are crucial and integral part of my life.

Not only those whom we met in school or college but also those who are present in every small and big part of problematic situation should respected.I learn a lot from mentors or guru's .and hoping to learn more from them."Not my all teachers are bad ;and those whom I labelled as 'bad' too have some good qualities" .For science and maths,I said them boring 'coz I don't like it.

People around me always emphasis on the importance of study it by advising me "maths need practice" . "try to solve more questions to gain more marks" and so on .I completely agree with them but you know I made a philosophy not good as Shakespeare but still........

"If you are interested in maths and science you can be
Stephen Hawking
But if you are reading it under pressure than you' ll become
Hawking pressure cooker"

Now I consider you smarter than me to understand everything which is unsaid by me...

Hoping for your love..

- Your Bohemian

Printed by Libri Plureos GmbH in Hamburg, Germany